Also by John Sager

A Tiffany Monday – an Unusual Love Story, West Bow Press 2012

Joan's Gallery, 50 Years of Artistry by Joan
Johnson Sager, Blurb, Inc. 2013

Uncovered – My Half-Century with the CIA, West Bow Press 2013

Night Flight, A Novel, Create Space, 2013

Operation Night Hawk, A Novel, Create Space, 2014

Moscow at Midnight, A Novel, Create Space, 2014

The Jihadists' Revenge, A Novel, Create Space, 2014

Mole, A Novel, Create Space, 2015

Capital Crises, A Novel, Create Space, 2015

God's Listeners, An Anthology, Create Space, 2015

Crescent Blood, A Novel, Create Space 2016

Sasha, from Stalin to Obama, A Biography, Create Space 2016

Shahnoza – Super Spy, A Novel, Create Space, 2016

Target Oahu, A Novel, Create Space, 2017

Aerosol, A Novel, Create Space, 2017

The Health Center, A Novel, Create Space, 2017

The Conservator, A Biography, Create Space, 2017

The Evil Alliance, A Novel, Create Space, 2018

Tehran Revisited, A Novel, Archway Publishers, 2019

St. Barnabas, A Novel, Inspiring Voices, 2019

The Caravan, A Novel, Outskirts Press, 2019

Senator McPherson, A Novel, Inspiring Voices, 2019

Meetings in Moscow, A Novel, Outskirts Press, 2019

Madam President, A Novel, Outskirts Press, 2019

Kiwi Country, A Novel, Outskirts Press, 2020

Conquering Covid, A Novel, Inspiring Voices, 2020

COPING WITH
COVID

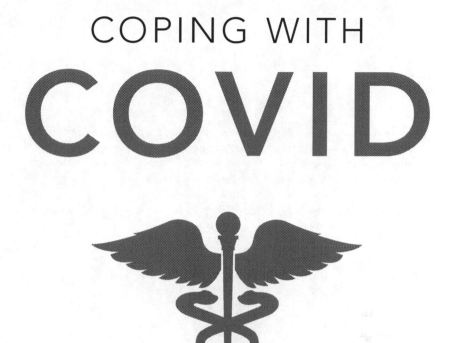

JOHN SAGER

InspiringVoices®

Inspiring Voices books may be ordered through booksellers or by contacting:

Inspiring Voices
1663 Liberty Drive
Bloomington, IN 47403
www.inspiringvoices.com
844-686-9605

ISBN: 978-1-4624-1322-5 (sc)
ISBN: 978-1-4624-1323-2 (e)

Library of Congress Control Number: 2020925830

Print information available on the last page.

Inspiring Voices rev. date: 02/12/2021

ACKNOWLEDGMENT

As with many of my stories, I want to thank my good friend and fellow fly fisherman Stanford Young. Stan and I are both in our nineties and no longer able to fish but we do have fond memories of when we were able to fish, together. Stan has perused every line of this work and where there are any typos, glitches or other mistakes, they are mine, not his. Thank you Stan!

AUTHOR'S NOTE

This is a sequel to the earlier work, *Conquering Covid*. As readers might understand, the experimental vaccine was *not* as successful as had been hoped. Its manufacturer, *Covid Control*, after more than a year of trying, was forced to declare bankruptcy. While the experts searched for an effective vaccine, the world's population struggled to adapt.

What follows are some examples of that struggle.

ONE

Hunt's Point, home to some of the Pacific Northwest's wealthiest and most influential citizens, is a nearly-private enclave jutting northward into Lake Washington, a few miles east of Seattle. A few of the homes at its northern extremity have their own swimming pools, even though a person can swim in Lake Washington, only a few steps distant. That would be true in the months of summer, but in other seasons Lake Washington's waters are too chilly for swimming. That is why many of these pools are heated: their owners can swim whenever they wish.

One of the families so blessed belongs to Harry Williamson III, the leading partner of Williamson, Garland, Smithson and White, Bellevue's oldest and most prestigious law firm. Williamson, at age 50, is probably the most capable—and feared—attorney in Washington state. A client can expect to be billed 400 dollars an hour for the firm's services, which is why nearly all of the firm's business comes from corporations and the city's largest retailers.

Despite the family's considerable wealth, Harry and his wife Marie decided that their only child—daughter Deborah—should attend Bellevue's public school system, rather than the few private schools that were available and easily affordable. Deborah—Debbie, as her many friends called her—had become a beautiful young woman, at 18 years Bellevue High's most attractive and sought-after female. Some of her friends, behind her back, spoke of her as a spoiled brat, beautiful, rich, and fearless. Most of this was pure jealousy. Debbie was smart and she already spoke passable French. But she was restless. Graduation was approaching, she hadn't yet decided on a career path and, most of all, she had not yet found 'Mr. Right.' She really didn't wat a career; she wanted to get married, have several kids, and let her husband do the rest.

As she thought about it, she decided she should invite some of her friends to her home. A few of them were facing the same uncertainties that bedeviled Debbie. It would be good to share ideas and, by inviting a few of her male classmates—especially her boyfriend, Jimmy Parsons—they could talk about their futures.

She was beginning to like Jimmy. He had already been accepted by the University of Washington, planning to get a degree in civil engineering. Those kinds of jobs, eventually, would guarantee a good salary, enough that she and Jimmy could live comfortably. But, hey, Jimmy was just a friend. Marriage was probably the furthest thing on his mind.

Enough daydreaming. Debbie had to persuade her mother that holding a party in their home would be okay. Mom had already spoken—more than once—about the dangers of people getting sick from this so-called Coronavirus, especially if too many people gathered in one place. But Debbie persisted, promising that her guests knew the rules about masks and social distancing.

Finally, after several days of this non-stop badgering, Debbie's mother gave in. 'Okay,' she said. 'Invite you friends but don't say I didn't warn you!'

* * *

Debbie sat down with her laptop and designed, and printed,15 invitations. Eight for the boys—one especially for Jimmy—and eight more for her girlfriends. First thing the next morning they were in the mail. Each invitation provided the details: next Friday, 5:30 to ten p.m. Come as you are but bring a swim suit. We'll gather in my downstairs rec room and, please don't tell my mom, but the bar is fully stocked and we can drink whatever we like!

Much to her surprise, her mother decided to visit a neighbor while the party was in train. Her father was on a business trip, meaning *No parental watching!*

Although she had learned to cook, Debbie insisted the evening meal be catered: slices of chilled, cooked ham, French fries, chilled asparagus tips in Bearnaise sauce, avocado slices with lemon juice, small glasses of champagne and Baklava for dessert.

Then, into the heated pool! Every guest had brought his/her swim suit, the girls showing off with the two-piece variety. Debbie's figure was the envy of all her guests. She waded to one side of the pool, the water up to the top of her shoulders. She motioned for Jimmy to come join her, which he did. As he snuggled up to her, he reached down with his right hand, between her skin and the swimsuit, found her stiffened nodule and began to massage it.

"Ahh! Oh, my God, Jimmy! That feels *so* good!! But let's wait until the others leave. Then we can go to bed and do it right!"

*   *   *

The home's downstairs rec room featured a well-stocked bar, a small dance floor, and two small adjoining bedrooms. As soon as the last guest left, Debbie took Jimmy's hand and led him into the nearest bedroom. The two lovers were so into each other than neither considered he should use a condom. The made love, twice, before falling asleep.

Early the next morning, Debbie was aware that her mother was sleeping, soundly, she hoped, in the family's upstairs bedroom.

She showed Jimmy the way to the nearest exit, kissed him goodbye and went back to bed.

An hour later, she showered, then went upstairs and found that her mother had prepared breakfast.

"How was your party, Sweetheart?"

"Oh, Mom, it was perfect! Everybody had a good time, everyone went for a swim, the meal was perfect, nobody drank too much and they all agreed we should do it again!"

* * *

Three months later Debbie has missed her menses, twice, and she knows she's pregnant. She has to tell her mother and, as the family is Catholic, she knows the 'rules' about abortion.

"Oh, Mom, I'm so ashamed. Yes, of course, Jimmy is responsible but I don't want to tell him. He really is a nice person and he doesn't have to live with the truth."

"That's okay, Sweetheart. We can do this quietly so that no one will know, not even your father. There's a doctor I know who can help. He's very discreet and he knows what to do. He knows we're a Catholic family, but that doesn't matter. His clinic is downtown, in the Medical Sciences building, so when you go there no one will know why. And, of course, I'll be there, waiting."

* * *

Dr. Morton Fisher, a licensed gynecologist, had managed the births of at least two hundred infants. His colleagues considered him one of the best but none of them was aware of his dirty little secret. He performed abortions, a procedure he abhorred, but he always believed that he was doing the mother a huge favor by aborting her child. His years of experience had taught him that the procedure was especially daunting for mothers of the Catholic persuasion. But he assured each one of his patients that no one, but *no one*, would know.

He gave these same reassurances to Marie Williamson, when she told him about her daughter Deborah. Not lost on him was the fact that this family was one of the most well-known and respected in the Puget Sound region. Still, family status be damned. The young woman needed an abortion and he was the man to perform it.

* * *

The procedure was accomplished without complications and Debora and her mother returned to their home. In three more weeks, no one would be the wiser. But as he was about to retire for the night, Morton Fisher knew there was something wrong. The next morning he was certain: Covid-19, the symptoms were unmistakable. He had to assume that he had been infected at his clinic, part of the city's health care system. Next question: is it possible that he passed the infection to Deborah Williamson, while performing the abortion? And should he say anything to the Williamson family? No, not yet. Why worry them about something that may never happen?

* * *

Dr. Fisher was lucky. Within ten days the symptoms had passed and he went about his business as though nothing had happened. But, not so with Deborah. The pathogens were at work in her unsuspecting body and it would be another ten days before she knew what had happened. And on day seven she and boyfriend Jimmy met at an after hours bar and had drinks together, followed by another romp in Debbie's bedroom.

Jimmy, a senior at Bellevue High and a member of the school's debate team, resumed his practice sessions with the team's coach, 40 year old Thelma Watson. The team had a scheduled competition with Newport High School and the participants— for reasons never understood—were not required to wear masks. The contest was a draw, the three judges awarding 60 points to each side, and the students returned to their classrooms, unaware that each of them was now infected by the novel Coronavirus.

* * *

One month later there were ten teenagers, five from Newport High and five from Bellevue High School, in Overlake Hospital's emergency care facility, each on a ventilator. After three days of 24/7 attention by the doctors and nurses, three were pronounced dead and were taken to the King County morgue. The other seven eventually recovered and returned to their homes.

The parents of the three deceased—Mr. & Mrs. James Clark, Mr. & Mrs. Donald Calhoon and Mr. & Mrs. Fred Boykin— filed a lawsuit in King County Municipal Court, accusing Debbie's parents of reckless endangerment by allowing the swimming party, at their home, where the Coronavirus infection chain began. The filing papers specified a request for punitive damages, two million dollars for each death, and one million each for pain and suffering, a total of $9,000,000.

For the first time in his nearly thirty years of law practice, Harry Williamson III found himself as a *defendant*. His three partners assured him that he could probably persuade the jury to reduce the penalties by at least one-third but Harry wasn't so sure.

Jury selection dragged on for nearly a month and by that time Seattle's television and newspaper reporters were in a feeding frenzy, interviewing any and everyone who had any knowledge of what had happened.

* * *

The trial lasted only three days and when it was over the jury decided for the plaintiffs, awarding the entire $9,000,000, $3,000,000 to each of the three.

For Williamson and his wife there was only one solution: declare bankruptcy and move south to Portland, to join his brother's law firm. Their Hunt's Point mansion eventually sold for $4,500,000, including the family's two Mercedes automobiles.

As the last piece of furniture was loaded into the Beacons moving van, the family housekeeper, Gretta Brestel, decided to take one last look at the surroundings she had come to love. The home was now empty, as were the two garages. What about the pool?

Gretta walked to the pool's edge and to her horror saw what she knew to be Debbie Williamson's naked body, lying at the bottom of the pool with what appeared to be a bundle of steel rebar tied to her right ankle.

She was barely able to control her panic but she found her iPhone and tapped the 911 icon. Ten minutes later two Bellevue emergency response cars arrived. One of the drivers phoned the King County morgue, asking that a hearse be dispatched at once. The other driver told his colleague they might be witnessing a crime scene. Better go slow. First thing, get the King County medical examiner to put a hold on the hearse, to allow him to examine Debbie's body. Also, find the Bellevue police department's fingerprint expert. There might prints on the rebar.

* * *

"What do you think, Tom? Did this young woman take her life or did someone take it for her?"

"Fred, if it was murder whoever did it wanted it to *appear* as a suicide. We need to reach the young woman's parents. If the ME is going to do an autopsy, he'll need their permission."

* * *

Immediately after learning of his daughter's death, Harry Williamson returned to Bellevue and checked into a room at the Bellevue Hilton hotel. The next morning he met with the KC medical examiner, in his office, and detective Frank Baxter, he of the department's Criminal Investigations division.

"Dr. Jeffreys, last evening I phoned you permission to do an autopsy on my daughter. What, if anything, did you learn?"

"Uh, Mr. Williamson, this is likely to be troubling so I suggest we sit down. What I found was that there was *no* water in your daughter's lungs or stomach. That means she had died *before* she reached the bottom of your swimming pool. In other words, Sir, she was murdered. Whoever did this wanted it to appear as a suicide, which explains the rebar strapped to her ankle. She would have had to add extra weight to take her to the pool's bottom. Unfortunately, there were no fingerprints on the rebar so we really have no idea who might have done this."

"Mr. Baxter. I know for sure that my daughter did *not* take her life! For one thing, she knew nothing about rebar, how it's used, where to find it. How many places sell that stuff? Construction supply houses, others?"

"I was thinking the same thing, Mr. Williamson. And I know that McClendon's Hardware, in Renton, sells rebar. As soon as we're through here, I'll drive down there and have talk with the manager."

* * *

"Okay, Mr. Baxter, I get it. Each of our sales records is right here in this computer. If there's been a recent sale of rebar, it should be here, somewhere.

"Yeah, here it is, ten days ago. The salesman was Walt Boykin. Walt's working in the lumber yard right now. I'll ask him to come to my office. You can talk there."

* * *

"Mr. Boykin. I'm Frank Baxter. I work out of Bellevue's Criminal Investigations division. Mr. Hansen tells me you sold some rebar to a customer, ten days ago. What can you tell me about that?"

"Hmmm. You know, at the time I thought there was something fishy going on. The guy talked as though he's mentally retarded, kind of stumbled around; then he said he wanted 35 pounds of rebar and he asked me to cut it into 18 inch lengths. Claimed he was making an anchor for his boat, that he fishes for bass in Lake Washington. So I did what he asked, wrapped the bundle with bailing wire. Then, when he got to the checkout counter he paid cash, no credit card. So we don't have a name."

"What about your security cameras?"

"Yeah, that's a real possibility. They cover the parking lot and we might have a picture of him and his vehicle. With a license plate number you should be able to ID the guy."

* * *

At Bellevue's CI office, from one of its computer printers:

Washington license plate A356927, 2010 Chevy pickup truck, owner Gustav Trofimov, 4307 Burlington Avenue, Bellevue, Washington; phone 206 743 2269.

* * *

Frank Baxter is speaking to his supervisor, Sgt. David Millhouse.

"Dave, do we have a phone number for that Harry Williamson? He said he was moving to Portland to join his brother's law firm."

"It's right here in my phone: 503 368 3308."

After the third ring

"Mr. Williamson? This is Frank Baxter, Bellevue Criminal Investigation. Yes, that's right. Sir, I'm pretty sure we know who killed your daughter. If you'd be willing to come to my office, we could talk about it. - - - Good, thank you, Sir. See you tomorrow, three p.m."

* * *

In Baxter's office

"Sir, I know this is difficult for you but if you'll let me explain, I'm pretty sure you'll feel better."

"Okay, Sergeant, go ahead."

"It goes back to the rebar that was strapped to your daughter's right ankle. We know the killer wanted everyone to believe that she had committed suicide, by drowning herself in your pool.

"We found the dealer who provided that rebar and he was able to help us identify the man who bought it. We've checked with Washington's Department of Licensing and we have the man's name, address, phone number *and* photograph.

"Here's an enlargement of that photo. Do you recognize the face?"

"I do. His name is Gustav Trofimov. He came to my office some time ago and wanted my firm to represent him. Said he had been accused of raping a young Black girl but he claimed he was innocent. He said that if she'd been raped, then somebody else must have done it.

"I asked him to step into our waiting room and while he was doing that I checked my computer files. I could tell he was retarded so I looked for the state's mental hospitals and I found his name—and the same photograph—at Western State Hospital in Lakewood. He'd been discharged a week earlier with the notation that he'd probably have to come back."

"Okay, so far, so good. But why do you think he killed your daughter?"

"Yes. I remember; he became very angry when I told him we would not represent him. He got up, stomped out of my office and shouted something like, 'You'll be sorry!'"

"So that seems to establish a motive. He wanted to 'get even?'"

"I believe so."

"Do you have any idea how he was able to find you daughter?"

"Hmmm, maybe. His name is Trofimov, right?"

"Yes."

"Okay, that that's a Slavic name, probably Russian. And the driver I employed—Anatoly Maxim—is also Russian, although now he's an American citizen. I'd bet a lot of money that these two men knew each other. Anatoly probably told Gustav a lot about me and my family. And what better way to 'punish' me and my family than to kill my daughter?!"

* * *

Gustav Trofimov was remanded to the Western State Hospital in Lakewood. After a week of intensive interrogations by officers of the Washington State Patrol, he confessed to killing Deborah Williamson. He had done so with the help of a friend who is still at large. The two men were able to force Deborah onto a bed, face down, then tied her hands behind her back. Her screams were stifled when Trofimov pulled a small plastic bag over her head, drew the drawstrings closed and the waited while she suffocated. They had talked about raping her (she was naked) but decided against it. Trofimov then attached the rebar package to her right ankle and the two men tossed her limp body into the pool.

*   *   *

King County Superior Court Judge Thomas Atkins told Trofimov that he was entitled to a trial by jury, but that, as he had already confessed, such a trial would produce the same result.

Trofimov is serving a life sentence, without the possibility of parole, at the Washington State Penitentiary in Walla Walla.

TWO

Harvey Mason is a 42 year old cattle rancher, with a large spread in Yellowstone County, Montana. An only child, he was born in Butte, later took a degree in agriculture science from Montana State University in Bozeman and at age 24 bought his first head of cattle, two two-year old Herefords. At the time he was still living with his parents and with his father's help he sold at auction the two Herefords for $3,500 each, giving half of that back to his father. He knew that the Hereford is America's favorite source of prime beef, so why not stay with that same animal? Without saying so, Henry Mason knew that his son was a budding entrepreneur, someone who—some day—would become one of the wealthiest men in all of Montana. And with wealth comes influence. One of Montana's two senators, Republican Jeremy Anderson, was a good friend of Henry Mason and in the United States congress he consistently pushed legislation that would favor the economies of Montana, Idaho and Middle America.

But then, the Coronavirus epidemic began its onslaught, not only in Montana but throughout the rest of the nation. It would impact the Mason family as it would most others.

What follows is part of that story.

* * *

Harvey Mason parked his Ford pickup truck in the driveway, kicked off his dirty boots, stomped through the back door into the kitchen, yanked open the fridge door, grabbed a bottle of Heineken's and sat down. ' Where the hell is Marie?', he asked himself. He was as angry as he could remember and he needed to vent. His wife was a good listener and she had a way with her husband.

"What's wrong, Sweetheart? You look as though you've been robbed!"

"Pretty much the same thing, Marie. I'm just back from that auction I told you about. I used the large hauler and offloaded fifteen of our Hereford two-year olds; that leaves us with sixty more, grazing out there on the back forty.

"Then the damned auctioneer started the bidding at $3,500 for each animal when everybody there knew $3,900 was the right figure. So, I finally settled for $3,700, splitting the difference."

"Hmm, that's almost $56,000, much more than enough to pay for Jeff's room, board and tuition. Butte's School of Mines Web page says that about $22,250 should be enough for one year, so if you sent it all to Jeff, that would be enough for two years!"

"Yeah, you're right, as usual. His latest email said he's been accepted as an entering freshman. His first courses are part the school's deep mining curriculum and as soon as I wire him that money, he's good to go. There's an old saying that Butte is a mile high and a mile deep, referring to the copper and silver mining that's been going on there for nearly a century, and coal, too. But Jeff's interest is in fracking; one of his professors told hm this is where the petroleum industry's future lies and Jeff wants to be part of it."

"Do we know anything about the school's rules for avoiding the Coronavirus? Social distancing, masks, that sort of thing?"

"Yes, we do. I spoke with Jeff the other day. He and his roommate—a freshman from Seattle—are required to wear a mask whenever they're together in their room, except when they're going to bed for the night. His dormitory's bathrooms have warning signs, 'Wash your hands, *thoroughly*, and use the hand sanitizer fluid after each washing.'

"The school's cafeteria has similar rules. At the tables, chairs are spaced six feet apart, everyone going through the chow line has to wear a mask; those who refuse are told to leave. Same in the kitchen; everyone wears a mask and the kitchen's refuse is burned, not sent to a landfill."

"Well, I think I feel better, knowing what you've told me. Jeff's expecting me to call in an hour and I'll tell him."

"How much does Jenny know about this? Those twins have never had a single secret between them. She'd be really upset if she thought we're holding back."

"You're right, but not to worry. She's coming over later this afternoon for coffee and conversation, as she likes to say. The hospital gives each of its nurses a half-hour break and with her electric scooter she can be here in five minutes."

"Yeah, she's turned into quite a young lady. The hospital's management allowed her to sign on as an intern so it'll be a few more years before she qualifies as a licensed nurse. Even so, at age 23 she's a real beauty!"

"Beauty *with* brains, Sweetheart. We've never talked about it but I'm pretty sure she's still a virgin. Still looking for Mr. Right, that's my guess."

*　*　*

Jenny Mason's workday ended at 3:30. She was dead tired after ten hours on the job, something the hospital's management had arranged after its negotiations with the nurses' union failed to reach a settlement for fewer hours and a ten percent increase in pay. At age 23 she was the hospital's newest hire and at the bottom of the institution's pecking order, something she resented but could do nothing about. To add to her angst, her boyfriend had tried to get her to go to bed on their most recent date. Sam Dawkins, the son of the hospital's administrator, thought he had a green light with Jenny. But she said absolutely not, slapped him hard, and stomped out of the hospital's rear entrance.

Now, she could hurry home and tell Mom what had happened.

* * *

"He what?!"

"That's right, Mom. It was closest thing to rape you could imagine! And I really like Sam, or I did. Now, I'm not so sure. And if I complain to the hospital's management, Sam's mother is likely to fire me."

"You know, Sweetheart, there are rules about this sort of thing. Montana has a law that parallels the federal law. Workplace harassment—especially if it's sexual—is a crime. Your father could file a lawsuit in the Billings Municipal Court and sue Sam Dawkins for sexual assault. If he's convicted, the fine could be as much as $50,000."

"What about publicity? I don't want my picture on television!"

"Look at it this way. Your father is one of the wealthiest and most influential men in Yellowstone County. He can see to it that there isn't any publicity. Matter of fact, he and one of the judges at the Yellowstone County courthouse are close friends.

As there are only three judges, I'm sure he could see to it that his friend hears your case".

* * *

The next morning

"No, Marie, that won't work. The moment I talk to judge Prescott he'll tell me to forget it. You and I both know how this goes; it's a he-said, she-said deal. No witnesses, zilch. I'm sorry, but you'll have to tell our daughter she'd best try to get along with Sam Dawkins. He's not a bad guy, the two might even be able to get along."

"Okay, Harvey, I'll tell her what you just told me. She won't like it but you're right. She probably *should* try to get along with Sam. She's smart enough to tell him how she feels, that she likes him but that doesn't include sex."

* * *

Later, Jenny meets Sam in the hospital cafeteria.

"Yeah, Jenny, as I thought about it, you're right. I'm ashamed of myself and I'm asking you to forgive me. We don't have to make a big deal out of this, but as we're both Lutherans, we know what Jesus said about forgiving others."

"Sam, that's the nicest thing you could say to me. Sure, let's forget the whole thing. How about that date we sort of had, going to that dance at the Northern Hotel?"

"My pleasure. I'll pick you up at six, we can have dinner and drinks before the dance. I've been there and the hotel's dining room is awesome; even has a small dance floor. And on Friday and Saturday evenings they have a five-piece orchestra."

*   *   *

The orchestra was everything they hoped it would be. Smooth, danceable, music, some swing but mostly current dance tunes. Unexpected, though, each of the musicians was wearing a mask. And the dining room's tables were spaced at least six feet apart. No matter, she was pleasantly surprised to learn that Sam was a very good dancer; he held her tight, but not *too* tight. And he paid for their sumptuous meal with a credit card, probably his father's but she didn't ask. The drive home, in Sam's five-year-old Mercedes convertible, was a perfect way to end their evening: top down, a full moon and shirt-sleeve weather. She decided to let him kiss her goodnight, a sort of signal: let bye-gones be bye-gones.

"Thanks, Sam, that was a perfect evening. I hope we can see more of each other."

"Jenny, you can count on it!"

THREE

During her sophomore year at Montana State University, Jenny Mason—with welcome encouragement from her parents—decided to compete for a vacancy in the university's School of Nursing. The entry exams were tough, but she completed them with a B-plus average, good enough for her to apply for a position at the Martin Luther Memorial Hospital in downtown Billings. Now, after a two-year internship, Jenny has her license as a registered RN. She's still the most junior person on the hospital's staff, but she's been assigned to the hospital's Emergency Care unit.

The unit treats mostly elderly—Medicare—victims of house fires, car crashes, rarely a patient with gunshot wounds and, most recently, it has admitted three patients who have been diagnosed with Covid-19. The hospital's administrator, Dr. William Montague, only recently received permission from the Montana state Board of Health, to install three ventilators, at the cost of $5,000 each. It was no secret that Dr. Montague's friendship with Republican Senator Orville Anderson was the key to getting the money.

As one of three nurses, it's Jenny's shared responsibility to ensure that each of the Covid patients receives 24/7 care and part of her routine is to visit each of the three at the beginning and end of each of her shifts. While doing this she follows the hospital's rules: she wears a mask and Latex gloves and changes her sterilized gown before and after each visit.

Then, the unexpected. Jenny awakens one morning with a throbbing headache, sore muscles, coughing and chills, the urge to vomit—the sure symptoms of Covid-19. She phones the hospital and is told to stay home and self-quarantine for two weeks. Somewhat to her surprise, after day ten the symptoms have disappeared and she believes she's now immune to the disease. She reports this to the hospital and its administrator asks her to come into the ER where she'll be tested to be certain her body is free of the Coronavirus pathogen.

The tests show that she's germ-free but the technician warns her that she can still pass the virus to others, i.e. wear a mask and practice social distancing when around other people.

* * *

Jenny and her mother are seated at the kitchen table- - -

"That's wonderful news, Sweetheart."

"Mom, no kidding. I was scared to death. I've never been so frightened. I was convinced I was going to die."

"Well, you're okay. What about going back to work?"

"Yes. The hospital says it's okay and I'll get my old job back, just like it was before."

"I have a surprise for you, if you haven't heard already."

"No, what is it?"

"Your brother is coming home for a visit!"

"Oh, that's wonderful! It'll be *so* good to see him again."

"He said he can stay only three days. His courses at Butte's School of Mining are more difficult that he expected. He'll probably bring his laptop so he can study while he's here."

"He wants to learn more about fracking?"

"Yes. He says this method of oil and natural gas extraction has made our country the world's leading producer of petroleum energy. And he sees a bright future for himself, as soon as he's able to 'join the team,' as he puts it."

"You know, Mom, I've been thinking it would be a good idea for me to introduce Jeff to Sam Dawkins. They're about the same age and Jeff should know that I'm dating Sam."

"I don't see why not. Sure, go ahead. Tell you what. You arrange it just as you said and I'll fix Jeff's favorite dinner; medium rare prime rib beef, mashed potatoes with gravy, half an avocado with mayo and a glass of California Merlot. The dining room's table is big enough. It'll be old home week for Jeff and Sam can see how we do things as a family."

*   *   *

Jeff Mason decided to drive, rather than take the Greyhound bus. He figured he could get from Butte to Billings in about an hour and a half, so long as his beat-up ten year old Toyota held together. Fortunately, Interstate 90 was clear of snow through the mountain pass near Butte, and he arrived home just in time for dinner. Jenny heard his car as it entered the driveway. She rushed out to meet him, threw her arms around him and the twins hugged each other as though they'd been separated for years.

"Hey there, Sis. Easy does it!"

"Oh, Jeff, we're so proud of you!. Come on in, Mom's waiting. You go to your room, change, and when you're ready we'll have dinner together. I'll phone Sam Dawkins and he'll join us."

"Who's Sam Dawkins?"

"Sam and I are dating. His mom is the administrator of the hospital where I work. You'll like him, I'm sure."

"Not to be nosey, but how serious is this?"

"I think Sam would like it if we got married, but he's never asked me and I'm not sure I'd say 'yes,' even if he did."

"Well, okay, if you say so. But I don't want Sam or anyone else fooling around with my sister."

"Honestly, Jeff, he did try to take me to bed but I said No Way. I told Mom and the two of us decided it's best if Sam and I try to be good fiends, no more than that ."

*   *   *

The dinner was a huge success and after Jeff and his sister loaded the dishwasher everyone retreated to the family library. In their excitement, no one remembered to don a face mask. Jenny thought about mentioning it but decided not to.

"So, Jeff, how's it going at school?"

"Pretty well, I'd say. Although there's something going on that makes me wonder."

"Such as?"

"Yeah. There's this young woman, her name is Tanya Morozova. She's a Russian exchange student. She's very attractive, about my age, and she claims she wants to learn more about how fracking works in the United States.

"I've talked to her about this and she says the Russians are skeptical about fracking. They say it's bad for the environment and they want no part of it. She told me her father is an official at the Russian embassy in Washington. He's an accredited diplomat and she's here on one of those exchange student visas. That means she can stay here as long as she stays in school and her grades are good enough."

"You sound like you're suspicious."

"Of course I'm suspicious! You would be, too, if you thought about it. Look, everybody knows that the US of A is the world's leader in the production of oil and natural gas and our fracking methods are largely responsible. My guess is that his woman wants to learn as much as she can about how we do it so she can report all this technical info to her government.

"What's more, I told the FBI office in Butte about this woman and three days later they told me that her father is a Russian intelligence officer and that he's almost certainly using his daughter as an agent."

* * *

What Jeff Mason did NOT tell his friends is that his FBI contact asked him if he'd be willing to 'cozy up' to the Morozova woman and try to learn more, even if it meant developing a romantic relationship. Jeff said 'Yes,' signed a secrecy agreement and is now is a security-cleared FBI informant.

FOUR

Jeff is taking a break from one of his classes and walks into the school's cafeteria. He sees the Morozova woman sitting by herself, drinking a cup of coffee.

"Hi, may I join you?"

"Uh, sure. And you can remove your mask. I have."

"Thanks. Say, I haven't seen you before. What's your name?"

"Tanya. Tanya Morozova. I'm Russian, as you can probably tell from my accent, but---

"No, no, your English is okay."

"Well, thanks, it's nice of you to say that."

"It's none of my business but what are you doing here, in Butte, of all places?"

"Yes, I don't blame you for asking. I'm an exchange student. I have a degree in petroleum engineering from Moscow State University and I'm doing graduate work here to learn more about fracking, the way you Americans do it. You may not know it, but Butte's School of Mines is well known in my country."

"How long to you plan to stay?"

"My visa is good for one year and that should be enough. I'm pretty good at what I do; that's why I was chosen to come here."

"Family?"

"Sure. My father is a diplomat, he's assigned to the Russian embassy in Washington, DC. My mom died some years ago and so he's a widower and I'm an only child. And, truth be told, mine is a lonely life. Butte is not an attractive city and it's hard to make friends here."

"Well, Tanya, you now have at least one friend, me. If you're not busy this evening we can go to a place I know in downtown Butte. It's called Barney's Bar and Restaurant. Barney has a five piece orchestra and a small dance floor. And the food is very good."

"I could say yes, but you haven't told me your name."

"Oh. Sorry about that. It's Jeff, Jeff Mason."

* * *

Jeff phoned ahead for reservations and he and Tanya are seated at a table in the far corner of the dining room. The orchestra has begun to play.

"I should warn you, Tanya, I'm not much of a dancer. How about you?"

"You're probably unaware, Jeff, but every Russian girl I know dreams of becoming a ballerina. If you're good enough to perform on-stage, the pay is quite good. I'm no exception; I began taking dancing lessons when I was seven years old. I was never good enough to become a ballerina but I do love to dance."

"What kind of music? Are you particular about that?"

"No, Silly, of course not."

"You ever hear of Glenn Miller?"

"I believe so, yes."

"They're playing his most famous piece, *Moonlight Serenade*. It's what we call 'Slow Swing.' I think even I can dance to that one. Want to try?"

* * *

Jeff found Tanya to be 'light as a feather' on the dance floor. Within a few bars they were cheek to cheek, as though it was the most natural thing. He sensed that Tanya had no fear, she was enjoying it as much as he.

"Hey, not bad, wouldn't you say?"

"I loved every minute of it, Jeff, thank you."

"Tanya, the orchestra is about to take a break. We should order dinner. This is on me, so feel free to order whatever you like."

"Yes. I see they have beef stroganoff. That's a popular item in Russia and here, too, if I'm not mistaken. At home we eat it with *smetana* or what you call sour cream. And it goes well with most any green vegetable, here they have asparagus tips in *sauce bearnaise*. So that's what I'd like."

"To drink?"

"Yes. But we need to be careful. A vodka martini would be nice, with a California Merlot following. But you're driving. What to you think?"

"I'm not worried, Tanya. I'll get you home safely, I promise."

* * *

The FBI office in Butte was a small one, with only two Special Agents assigned, a communications clerk and a secretary. Donald Clark was the one to whom Jeff Mason reported his contact with the Morozova woman. The next morning, after delivering Tanya Morozova safely to her quarters, Jeff walked into Clark's office.

"Mr. Clark, we need to talk about Tanya Morozova."

"It's Don, Jeff, go ahead."

"Okay, Don. Here's what I think is happening. Tanya *asked* me to kiss her goodnight and, even though we both were a bit high, I think she'd be happy to crawl into bed with me. So this has become far more than a friendship and that bothers me."

"How so, Jeff?"

"Put yourself in my shoes. You've asked me to feed her a bunch of info that she's sure to report to her father in Washington. *Disinformation*, I believe you guys call it. That means you expect me to *lie* to her and I'm not sure I can do that; not with a clear conscience."

"I get that, Jeff, but what you need to consider is the value of what we're asking you to do. If this plan succeeds it will send the Russian government into panic mode. Their currency will lose value almost overnight, their oil and natural gas income will plummet, the government might have to default on its loans. What we have here is an opportunity to seriously destabilize the Russian government.

"I'm not at liberty to tell you *how* we arranged this but take my word for it, this operation has the approval of the FBI director in Washington, and, yes, the White House."

"Well, okay. Knowing that I suppose I can go ahead with your plan. But you need to give me the details, okay?"

* * *

Readers may be forgiven for not remembering a major happening in the life of Jeff Mason. Recall that when Jeff drove into the family driveway—after his brief drive from Butte—his sister rushed out to greet him, giving him a bear-like hug. In that brief moment, the Coronavirus pathogen passed to Jeff. He is now unaware but has become what is know as an asymptomatic carrier, *meaning that he can pass the pathogen to others without knowing it. And so it was that when Tanya Morozova asked Jeff to kiss her goodnight, she became infected.*

Ten days later, Jeff and Tanya are seated in the school's cafeteria.

* * *

"Tanya, I don't know what you think of American politics but every four years we elect, or re-elect, a president. The television channels show a map of the United States. Those states that traditionally vote for the candidate of the Democratic Party are colored blue. The Republican-leaning states are red."

"Yes, I believe I read about that somewhere."

"What you may not know is that Montana has been a red state for many years. Like all states, Montana sends two senators to Washington but only one representative, because of our small population. It so happens that the senior senator from Montana, Arthur Ashford, is a good friend of my father. My father is one of the wealthiest men in the state and he routinely contributes heavily to Ashford's campaign. The two men have become close friends and Ashford tells my father things that he probably shouldn't.

"Me, I really don't care. But what my father told me the last time I saw him really frightens me and you should know why."

"Why should you be frightened?"

"Because senator Ashford is on the Senate's Foreign Relations Committee; in fact he's the vice-chairman. He told my father that there is a bill in his committee, about to be forwarded to the White House, that will place an embargo on all Russian shipments of oil and natural gas. That means your country's export earnings will drop by as much as 80 percent. The bill also has what is known as a 'sweetener,' an offer to all members of the European Union to buy American oil and natural gas at a thirty percent discount. The intent, as you can probably guess, is to virtually destroy the Russian economy. It's no secret that the leader of your country has openly expressed his hatred of the United States. It's what we call 'hard ball politics,' Tanya, and I don't like it one bit.

"But, please, tell your father about this. He needs to know. Perhaps he can do something to forestall the outcome."

*   *   *

Ten days later Jeff and Tanya are again seated in the school's cafeteria. Tanya is visibly upset.

"What is it Tanya? You've been crying."

"Jeff, about three weeks ago, I woke up feeling terrible, so I went to the hospital's emergency room. After some tests the doctor told me I have Covid-19. He ordered me to self-quarantine for two weeks and to avoid contact with other people. That's why I'm wearing the mask. I don't want you to catch it."

"Not to worry, Tanya. I'm sure you'll be just fine." (Jeff strongly suspects it was the goodnight kiss that infected Tanya but he decides not to mention it.)

"What makes it worse is that I've never told my father about your warnings about the Russian economy. It just seemed too awful and I didn't want him to worry."

*   *   *

A week later, Jeff receives a phone call from the hospital's administrator. Tanya Morozova died at three o'clock in the morning. She had been on a ventilator for three days but the Covid-19 infection could not be controlled. Jeff is stunned, overwhelmed with guilt. For the first time in his life, he drives to the nearest tavern, gets drunk and the proprietor finally sends him home in a taxi. The next day, after sleeping until noon, he calls FBI Special Agent Donald Clark and asks to see him later that day.

In Clark's office - - -

"As you know, Don, I was never very comfortable with that plan of yours, to feed all that disinformation bullshit to Tanya so she could pass it to her farther. Well, the poor woman died yesterday, from Covid-19, and I'm probably the guy who gave it to her. So you can tell your buddies at the FBI headquarters in Washington to go to hell. The plan didn't work and I couldn't be happier about that."

FIVE

Seattle Times outdoor reporter Tom Robinson has just arrived home from his monthly meeting with Seattle's Washington Fly Fishing Club. He's about to share his good fortune with his wife, Sally.

* * *

"Hey, Sally, I'm home and I've got great news!"

"You mean they agreed?"

"Yep. The board voted six to nothing in favor of my proposal."

"Oh, Tom, that's great news! When do we leave?"

"Well, we can go any time but the club will only pay for my travel, not yours. The contract calls for me to write one article each week, to be sent by FAX from New Zealand to the *Seattle Times*, with a copy for the club's newsletter, *Creel Notes*.

The board argued about whether we should go first class or coach but I told them we can afford to make up the difference, so we'll go first class."

"Sweetheart, I used my laptop to find Air New Zealand's schedule. They don't fly out of Seattle, so we'll have to connect in San Francisco. Like all the other airlines, they've cut back their schedule, and the Boeing 787 Dreamliner will carry only a half load. That allows for the social distancing that all the carriers require. So, in first class there won't be more than twenty passengers and everyone has to wear a mask."

"That means a stopover in Honolulu, and from there nonstop to Wellington?"

"Yes. But again, when do we leave?"

"One week from today. That will give me time to clean out my desk at the office and I need to update my fly fishing stuff. And I can do that for you, too, if you like."

"I think we have everything we need. Two fly rods for each of us, vests, waders, boots and a wading staff. Tell you what, I can pack all the stuff in a no-break container, we send it to Sea Tac's shipping department and we're all set."

* * *

New Zealand is a long way from Seattle, nearly half way around the globe. During the stopover in Honolulu Tom and Sally decided to order what the first class menu billed as 'Hawaii's Finest': two Mai Tai cocktails followed by a four-course dinner, with decaf coffee to finish. The Mai Tais did their job and the two slept all the way to Auckland.

Tom had negotiated a contract with Avis: a four-wheel drive 2018 Ford Explorer. He and Sally had read about Kiwi driving, everything backward from everywhere else: the steering wheel on the right side of the vehicle, among other nuisances. The Avis agent's final word of warning:

* * *

"Good luck, you two, and don't forget that *all* traffic is on the left side, both freeways and country roads."

"Thanks for the reminder. We'll be okay!

"Okay Sally, I'm the driver and you're the navigator. As I recall that road map tells us it's about 200 miles to Turangi which means we should get there in about four hours, maybe a little less."

"And Sam Jenkins knows we're coming?"

"Yes. I got his email address from the club and told him about when we'll be arriving. He sounds like a neat guy. He set up this fly fishing camp three years ago, limits the number of guests to no more than six at a time. The camp is right alongside the Tongariro River with three cabins and a separate office/

lounge/dining room where Sam lives and entertains his guests. According to this reservation, we'll be in Cabin Two. As you know, I've paid for the 'A' package which includes three meals a day, an hour of Sam's time each day—if we need it—and the use of one of his jet boats for moving up and down the river."

"You say 'If we need it.' What's that all about?"

"Sam is a licensed fly fishing instructor. Some of his guests have never fished before and he'll give them an hour or so of instruction, then serve as their guide until they get the hang of it. But any time a guest uses one of his jet boats, he insists on running it himself. That's a requirement of his liability insurance policy."

"What about other fishers in the river?"

"Yeah, that's an important question. Just like at home, we don't fish from the boat. We get out and wade. And if there are other fishers already there, we get in line, so to speak, maybe twenty yards behind. It can get complicated, too, because some fishers fish with nymphs and they cast *upstream,* not down. But either way, the protocol says that a fisher who enters the river behind someone who is already there, *must* maintain a distance of three casts; roughly, about sixty yards."

"And this is catch and release?"

"Absolutely. Just like back home, that means barbless hooks. I understand that all fly shops in New Zealand sell *only* barbless hooks. And if we have any that still have barbs, it's easy to pinch them down with a pair of needle nose pliers."

"You mentioned Zane Grey before I interrupted. Sorry."

"Yeah, he's a legend in these parts and for good reason, although few people our age know about this. In the 1920s and 30s he was the literary giant of his generation. He introduced the world to sport fishing in New Zealand. He first visited the country in 1926 and made three additional trips, all during the 'down under' summer months of December through March. The second was January to April 1927 and the third December 1928 to March 1929 and the last from December 1932 to February 1933."

"That's during the time of our Great Depression. He must have had a lot of money."

"He did, most of it from book sales. He set up a base camp at Otehei Bay in the Bay of Islands which soon became a destination for the rich and famous. He wrote articles that highlighted the uniqueness of New Zealand fishing and built a lodge and camp that was named the Zane Grey Sporting Club.

"Remember, too, that in those days the only way to get to New Zealand was by commercial sailing ships, and those trips took days. So it's safe to say that Zane Grey was as determined as he was successful."

"You talk about how great the fishing is in New Zealand. Are these fish native to the country or did they come from somewhere else?"

"Yeah, another interesting story. No, they're not native. Probably in the late 1800s there was a Kiwi entrepreneur, Jeffrey Mackenzie, a transplanted Scotsman, who wanted to set up a fish cannery, something he'd done years before in the North Sea's cold waters near his home in Edinburg. He'd done some research and decided to buy Rainbow Trout eggs from a cannery on California's Russian River. Anticipating the long haul to New Zealand, he packed those eggs in sawdust and ice, five barrels, and then planted them in several rivers, both South and North islands.

"As it happened, those rainbow trout soon grew to the six, seven, eight pounders that now inhabit those rivers that flow into the country's large lakes, Lake Taupo being the prime example. That lake is home to millions of tiny 'scrap fish,' the Kiwi's call them 'white bait.' They're minnow-size, no more than two inches long and that's what the Rainbow Trout feed on. Then, when it's time to spawn, they move into the rivers, like the Tongariro, spawn and then return to the lake.

"It's the same as with our steelhead in the Pacific Northwest, except those fish live in fresh water."

* * *

The two recognized the sign as soon as they saw it. Jenkins' Riverside Motel.

"That's it, Sally, and we're right on time. I see that our reserved parking spot is right where Sam said it would be. I believe that's him, coming out to greet us."

* * *

"You're Tom and Sally Robinson? Welcome to Turangi! You're in Cabin Two, right down there by the river. My house boy, Ari Parata, will take your luggage to your cabin. Ari's a Maori but completely trustworthy and his English is as good as yours and mine. You probably want to rest up before dinner, in a couple of hours. It so happens that you two are the only guests, for the next two days, so we can have dinner together And, I should remind you, we're required to wear a mask when moving around the grounds, but, mercifully, not while eating.

"In a few more days we'll be welcoming another fisher, Andrew Peterson. You may know him. He is, or was, a member of the Washington Fly Fishing Club. I understand his wife left him because he was fooling around with another woman. That makes no difference to me, so long as he's a reasonably good fly fisher and he pays for our services.

"Oh, one more thing. I presume that when you went through immigration at the airport, one of our health officers checked to make sure you're not carrying that virus bug."

"Yes, that's right. He told us we're good to go. And thanks, Sam. But we're pretty tired and a nap won't hurt."

*   *   *

Tom and Sally quickly changed into bathrobe and slippers and then noticed several brochures on the between-the-beds nightstand.

"Hey, Tom, look at this. It's a brochure telling visitors about New Zealand's approach to the Coronavirus pandemic. There's a picture here of their Prime Minister, Jacinda Ardern; says she's the leader of the country's Labour Party and she describes herself as a Social Democrat and a Progressive. Back home we'd say she's a Liberal Democrat, but not here, apparently."

"Yes, we've read about her. For one thing, she's persuaded her parliament and other government leaders to be serious about preventing the spread of the Coronavirus. When the disease first appeared here, in early January, she ordered a nationwide lockdown: schools, restaurants, bars and other public gathering places."

"Does anyone know how the virus got here?"

"Yes. A hospital in Wellington determined that a Chinese tourist had arrived at the Wellington airport on January 5. He checked into a motel and the next day turned himself in to a hospital. He was suffering from Covid-19 but at that time no one knew what it was, only that there were reports coming out of China about some kind of new disease that was spreading throughout the country. He was sent to the hospital's ICU where he died three days later. But, and here's the scary part, two of the ICU nurses were infected. Fortunately, they both recovered but by now the virus was starting to move. And that's when the prime minister made her decision.

"Within three months, New Zealand had the lowest rate of infections and deaths of any country on the planet, and she gets credit for most of that. Most of the citizenry love her, even those who don't share her political views."

"Well, I suppose it's good to know that Ms Ardern wants us all to stay healthy. But I *won't* be healthy if I don't get some sleep! It's nap time. How about you?"

SIX

Patti Murphey is a 32 year old prostitute who owns and operates her own brothel in White Center, a run-down suburb located a few miles south and west of downtown Seattle. Her brothel, known to its regular customers as Patti's Pad, is located in the basement of an abandoned warehouse on one of White Center's side streets. The local police know where it is and what it does, but Patti has an arrangement whereby she shares 20 percent of the take from each customer with the White Center precinct captain.

At the outset of the Coronavirus epidemic, Patti changed the rules for each of her customers. In addition to the requirement that each of them use a condom, she insisted that each of them sign a document attesting that they were virus free, insofar as they knew.

One of Patti's most glamorous hookers was Irene O'Sullivan, she of Irish extraction and with a figure that would stop traffic. Irene 'worked' for Patti only three nights a week: Thursdays, Fridays and Saturdays and she soon became the favorite of one Andrew Peterson. Why? Because with a little practice the two discovered they could reach orgasm at the same time. From then on, Andy made sure that when he visited Patti's Pad, Irene would be available.

What Andy did not know about his favorite hooker: Irene had a part-time job at a White Center tavern, Luigi's Lounge, where customers came and went without wearing masks. One evening while serving one of Luigi's customers, the man sneezed and those miniscule droplets entered Irene's mouth and nose. Neither of them knew it at the time but that customer was an asymptomatic carrier of the Coronavirus. The chain was predictable: Irene is infected and now so is Andy and neither of them is aware.

*   *   *

A few more words about Andy. He is a former member of the Washington Fly Fishing Club. Andy had been asked to resign his membership when the club's president learned that Andy had been patronizing Patti's Pad. As if that weren't bad enough, Andy's wife filed for divorce within hours of learning of her husband's indiscretions. Fortunately for Andy, his deceased father left him a generous trust fund, so money won't be a problem.

But Andy, if nothing else, is a persistent guy. He decided to leave his troubles behind and go to New Zealand, a place he knew to have some of the best fly fishing opportunities anywhere.

* * *

Andy has just checked in at the Jenkins' Riverside Motel. It is only by coincidence that he soon recognizes Tom and Sally Robinson and he wonders if they know why he was asked to resign his membership in the WFFC.

"Hey, Tom, fancy meeting you here!"

"Likewise, Andy. It's good to see you again. You remember Sally?"

"Certainly. The best lady fly fisher in the club!"

"How long do you plan to be here?"

"My reservation is for two weeks but I can extend it if I want."

"By the way, I presume you were tested at the airport, like everyone else?"

"Yeah. It didn't take long and I didn't like it. The guy who did the test told me he thought there might be a problem, but the test was 'inconclusive' so he let me pass."

"That's good news, Friend. How about we have dinner together?"

"Fantastic. Let's do it."

* * *

As his business grew, Tom Jenkins decided he should hire at least one guide, someone who knew the river, where and when the fish were likely to be found. He interviewed three applicants and settled on Charlie Williams, an experienced fly fisherman and already a licensed guide. Tom knew that Charlie was dating a Maori woman but decided the arrangement wouldn't make any difference. Tom knew that most Maoris were prone to drink too much and, much like the native Americans back home, were easily victimized by too much alcohol.

The contract was simple enough. Thirty-five kiwi dollars per hour for each hour on the river and Charlie can keep any tips that might come his way. So why not assign Charlie Williams to his newest client, Andy Peterson?

* * *

Both client and guide agreed it was a winning combination. Within 15 minutes of stepping into the river, Andy brought to hand an eight-pound Rainbow trout. The barbless hook came out easily and he was ready for another battle.

"Hey, Charlie, let's try the Major Jones pool. That's supposed to be one of the best on the river."

"You're the boss, Andy. If there's no one in the pool you can have your way with it."

True to form, Major Jones held three Rainbows, the smallest of which was six pounds. Andy hooked and released a seven pounder.

"Okay, Charlie. That's enough for one afternoon. I should quit while I'm ahead. By the way what are you doing this evening?"

"Yeah, I should be so lucky. I have a date with my girlfriend, Kala Henari. She's Maori, of course, 27 years old, beautiful and still single. I'll let you know all about it tomorrow."

*   *   *

The Coronavirus plays no favorites. Andy Peterson, the unaware asymptomatic carrier passed the virus to his guide Charlie Williams and he, during their sexual encounter, infected his Maori girlfriend, Kala Henari. There is some evidence that suggests that indigenous Maori men and women are more susceptible to infection than the mostly-English stock that inhabit New Zealand. And as it happened, Kala Henari decided to visit her parents in Wellington, the nation's capital, where she passed the infection to them. Within days, the virus had spread throughout Wellington's sizable Mauri population and was beginning to infect others.

In near-panic mode, Prime Minister Jacinda Ardern ordered a temporary cancellation of all inbound flights by Air New

Zealand and other international carriers. She urged that all outgoing Kiwis be tested for the Coronavirus. Shipments of New Zealand wool were put on hold. Within twenty-four hours the Kiwi dollar lost eighteen percent of its value on the international exchanges.

In Turangi, Tom and Sally Robinson saw the handwriting on the wall. Their lives might be threatened and it was time to leave. Tom consulted his laptop and discovered that there was one Air New Zealand flight leaving for Honolulu the next afternoon and there were five tourist class seats still available. He used his credit card and secured the two reservations.

* * *

At last report the Robinsons were safely home in Seattle. Tom will be writing a number of articles for his newspaper, reminding readers that the world-wide Coronavirus pandemic is still alive and well and that it should be taken *very* seriously.

SEVEN

United States embassy, Moscow, Russia, 0900 hours, Friday. United States ambassador Richard Sheldon is leading his weekly staff meeting.

"Okay, people, listen up. We've just received a long message from Washington. Our State Department colleagues have some interesting ideas about how we might be able to help shed some light on how our Russian hosts are dealing with this Coronavirus epidemic. And the White House is in the loop. So we need to pay attention.

"Yes, Charlie. Go ahead."

"Mr. Ambassador, my guys are already talking to people. We don't have enough info yet for an official report, but we're getting close."

"How close?"

"Well, for example, Tom Whittaker has been visiting with the director of that polyclinic on Petrovsky Boulevard, a Dr. Lazarof. The clinic has fifty beds and four ventilators. The doctor admitted that he can't keep up with the Covid-19 patients. In the past ten days, seven of them have died. He knows Tom will enough to tell him that Putin's claims that the virus is under control are nonsense, and everyone working for him feels the same way."

"Hmm, interesting. Helen, what say you?"

"Yes, Mr. Ambassador. I've made friends with a nurse who's working the day shift at the Buyanov hospital, across the river in the Lenin Hills district. It's a large facility, one of Moscow's oldest and most respected. A few days ago she told me that the hospital's director, a Dr. Petrov, was denied permission to buy and install another ten ventilators

There's an office in the Ministry of Health that approves—or denies—these requests and word came back that the ministry's budget couldn't afford the purchase.

"That hospital has a separate wing for Covid-19 patients, and there are, or were, twenty-seven of them. The nurse, Valentina Stepanova, told me that because of the lack of ventilators, five of her patients died, in just one week!"

"Hmm, I think, based on what I've just heard, that we have enough for a report to the Department.

"But first, Dan Coates, you're working the St. Petersburg story. What's going on there?"

"Yes, Mr. Ambassador. I was there for five days, got back only yesterday, but the story is much the same. St. Isaac's Hospital is the largest, dates back to Nikita Khrushchev's time, in the 1960s. The hospital has some 400 beds, on four floors, and a 30-bed ICU. For the past two months or so, that ICU has had nothing but Covid-19 patients and as my source put it, 'they're dying like flies.' I didn't dare ask him for a precise count but I know he was telling the truth."

"Okay. I'm sure it's not lost on any of you that these sources know they're talking to an American official. And that tells me they *want* Uncle Sam to know what's going on in Mother Russia. They're likely fed up with Putin's claims that all is A-Okay and they want us and the rest of the world to know it.

"That's very good work, folks. I'll have our secretary write it up and send it to Washington."

* * *

Four days later, in the office Thomas Wilde, United States Secretary of State. He is speaking to his deputy, Julia Townsend.

"Julie, I believe this report from our friends in Moscow is spot on but, having said that, I'm troubled."

"How so, Tom?"

"Even though this report will go to the White House, think about how the info was collected."

"Yes, face-to-face meetings. With or without masks."

"Exactly that. We know very little about how the virus is moving around in Moscow, but we have to assume that it *is* moving. And in that cool, damp environment, it moves even more effectively."

"Yes, I think I know where you're going with this. Bring everybody home?"

"Yes. Although we'll need the Pentagon's permission to disband the embassy's military attaché group. And no doubt Congress will raise hell if we try to do this but I think it's the right thing to do. No matter what, it's not worth losing any of our officers out there. We'd still have consular representation in Vladivostok and Yekaterinburg and that should be good enough."

* * *

The United States Senate's Foreign Relations committee has 22 members; 12 Republicans and 10 Democrats. The Democratic minority leader, Shirley Purvis of Massachusetts, is considered by most political observers as the most ultra-left member of the 100 person body.

When Purvis learned of Secretary Wilde's intent to bring his officers home, she immediately asked her minority colleagues for a no-confidence resolution which, if accepted by the entire committee, would block Wilde's plan. In speaking to reporters about her action, she said it was due to her lack of confidence in Secretary Wilde's leadership, that Wilde's order should be rescinded or that he should resign.

This news rapidly made its way throughout Capitol Hill and then to the White House.

Senate majority leader, Republican Dennis McDougal, told his colleagues that the Purvis resolution was improper and non-binding and, further, that Republican president Owen Oglethorpe would oppose any such plan.

* * *

Now there are 38 American diplomats and 19 military officers each back in his/her hometown, spreading the truth about what is really going on in Putin's Russia. Whether or not these efforts will change America's relationships with the Russian Federation remains to be seen.

EIGHT

Bonner Springs, Kansas. High school principal Mark Evans is speaking to his assistant, Marie Whitworth.

"Marie, there's an email from the governor's office on my desktop's screen. Have you seen it?"

"Yes, Mark. It's a new set of instructions on how he wants the state to deal with the Coronavirus epidemic. Every school cafeteria manager is to insist that all students wear masks; those who refuse are to be denied service. And the tables and chairs have to be repositioned to ensure the social distancing rules are followed. Every school in the state has received the same message, grades one through twelve. It doesn't say anything about our universities."

"Yeah, that's smart politics. Leave it each school to develop its own rules for fighting the bug. But we need to tell Barney

Adams about this. He runs the cafeteria and he can pass the word to his employees."

"I'll do that right away."

"I guess the governor is leaving it up to each school to manage its athletic program. Our high school football team is scheduled to play seven games, beginning in late September. Turnouts begin the day after school opens, September 8. And with Don Markle as our starting quarterback, we have a good chance of winning them all."

"Scheduled, yes. But do you think the teams can practice and then play, with this epidemic all around us?"

"Good question, Marie. I attended a principals' conference last week, reps from every school in our district. We decided that players and coaches will be tested for Covid-19. There's a facility that does that right here in town. Testing once a week and—important—no later than ten a.m. on game day. If everyone tests negative, then the game goes on, if not we'll cancel. The kids don't like this but they do understand.

"We made another decision that our fans should appreciate. Traditionally, our games were played on Friday evenings, giving parents and friends an opportunity to come and watch the games. But because such gatherings are now prohibited, we're going to play Saturday mornings, beginning at nine o'clock. And they'll be televised."

*   *   *

Donald Markle, eighteen years old and captain of his school's football team, was in his senior year at Bonner Springs high school. He had acquired something of a reputation as a BMOC (Big Man on Campus). Not only was he the team's quarterback, he also was pulling a 3.6 gpa. He'd already been accepted to enroll at Kansas State University and as an entering freshman he intended to turn out for the Junior Varsity Wildcats football team. But Don didn't like the attention. By nature he was shy and somewhat withdrawn, until he walked into the locker room and suited up for practice.

His parents, Sam and Melinda Markle, were at first reluctant to let their son play football. They knew he'd be 'mixing it up' with his teammates where—they were certain—there'd be a lot of bad language floating back and forth, including taking the Lord's name in vain, not a good thing for their son who was being raised in the Lutheran faith.

Don's sister, Amy, a year older, had belonged to her church's Luther League program since she was a shy, young 13-year old. Now, at 19, she was leading a weekly charity program in her church's basement, collecting money and durable goods for distribution to the city's homeless shelters and an Alcoholics Anonymous center in the downtown area. She insisted that all participants come to the church wearing masks and most did, but not all.

* * *

The family's pastor, Gerald Bjornestad, was a third-generation Norwegian who still had family in Oslo. At age 30, and single, he was one of the youngest Lutheran pastors in the country. When he came to Bonner Springs he had just completed his seminary training in Minneapolis, where he committed to the Evangelical Lutheran Church in America, the most liberal of the several Lutheran denominations. His ordination soon followed.

His services were by-the-book Lutheran tradition. Holy Communion once a month, the other Sundays also devoted to scripture reading, hymns and a message from the pulpit. At the beginning of each service the congregation stood and recited the Apostles' Creed but on the fourth (or fifth) Sunday they recited the longer and more complex Nicene Creed.

Following each service, the members of Holy Trinity Lutheran Church gathered in the church basement for coffee, snacks and, usually, a hymn sing organized and directed by Abigail Jensen, a 75 year old widow who was thought to be the woman 'who called all the shots.' Abigail had been a member of the church since its charter was first accepted by the ELCA Board of Governors in Minneapolis. Two of her grandchildren were regular worshippers, Jimmy Calhoon,18 and his brother Alex, a year older.

Alex had already been in trouble with the law, having been arrested for trying to steal a digital camera from a Target department store. He admitted his guilt and was released to his parents with a warning that, if it happened again, he could go to the local juvenile detention center.

But not so with his brother, Jimmy. In his senior year, Jimmy decided to study chemistry, believing that—eventually— owning and operating a pharmacy would guarantee him a good living and a way to meet interesting people. And with the recent news that a vaccine was on its way, one that could put a stop to the Coronavirus pandemic, he believed that helping others—as Jesus had urged His followers to do—would guarantee him a most-satisfying career.

But Jimmy worried about his sister. Amy had grown to become an attractive young lady, something every boy in the congregation knew. At first she was reluctant to accept requests for dating, believing that whoever it was, he probably wanted sex more than just her company. So she refused and, unfortunately, gradually gained the reputation of being a stuck-up snob. But there was one boy, ever-so-shy 18 year old Harold Hopkins, who had a crush on Amy. The fact that he came from a Black family, living in one of the city's poorer neighborhoods, made it nearly impossible for him to connect with Amy. But after Harold had attended a few of Amy's church-basement gatherings, the two grew to like each other. Amy's Christian spirit told her she should treat Harold as anyone else, forget that he's a poor, Black kid 'from the other side of the tracks.'

What neither Amy nor Harold knew: Harold was an asymptomatic carrier of the novel Coronavirus. He had become infected while attending an informal prayer meeting, organized by other families in his neighborhood. And, no surprise, he passed the pathogen to Amy during one of their evening gatherings.

Three weeks later Amy told her parents that she wasn't feeling well and, she feared, her symptoms were all too familiar: sore throat, difficult breathing, fever and coughing.

* * *

"Mom, maybe if just stay home and in bed for a few days, I'll be better. What do you think?"

"NO, Sweetheart! I'm taking you to see Dr. Williamson. He has a Covid testing system right there in his office and the results are quickly available. If this IS Covid-19, then we—you, especially—need to know it."

"Well, okay, if you say so. Have you told dad?"

"Yes and he's told most of his farming friends at their recent Grange meeting. They're all very concerned, not just about you but what happens if the virus gets loose. Most of these men have large wheat or corn spreads and they're quite well to do. But money won't help if the infections begin to spread.

"What may be even worse, your father told me this morning that mayor Johnson is about to order a city-wide lockdown: close all the restaurants and bars, barber shops and beauty parlors; maybe, even, close all the K thru 12 schools and do the teaching with Zoom."

"What about our church services?"

"Yes. Pasto Bjornestad is sending word to all our church members that, until further notice, all services will be virtual. He'll call in the needed participants on Wednesdays, and our IT man will record the whole thing, to be broadcast at eleven o'clock on Sunday. Unfortunately, this means no more Luther League meetings or other gatherings in the church basement.

"But, look, Sweetie, you need to get better. Fortunately, your Covid case is relatively mild and the doctor says you'll recover and be as good as new. So plan on saying home and in bed for as long as it takes."

NINE

*American Embassy, Kabul, Afghanistan. CIA Chief of Station
Richard Lawson is speaking to his deputy, Arthur Waite.*

"So, Art, how'd your meeting go?"

"Not bad, Dick. Of course, he's walking on eggs, knowing what
would happen if he were found out. I haven't told him, but I
do believe he's convinced that he's the *only* penetration of the
Taliban that we have.

"I'm setting up a dummy file for the station and headquarters.
It will contain his real name—Amin Kalhan—but we'll assign
a cryptonym, something like ZYCOBRA."

"What did he have to say?"

"Yeah, very interesting, and telling. A few days ago he attended
one of his weekly meetings, run by the chief of his six-man

group, a guy he knows only as Mullah Javid. That's not his real name and everybody knows it. This Javid guy told them that the entire organization, throughout Afghanistan, is celebrating the news out of Washington."

"I can guess why."

"Yep, our mercurial president Owen Oglethorpe says he's going to bring most of the American troops home, in time for Christmas. According to yesterday's *Wall Street Journal,* this is a very bad idea. One of its editorials reminds readers that Oglethorpe promised to 'stop these endless wars' as part of his campaigning in 2016. We're also reminded that the president's military advisors, including most of the generals in the Pentagon, have warned him that if he follows through, the Taliban will have a field day, not just here but in Pakistan, too."

"What if Oglethorpe fails to overturn the election? He's still trying."

"I understand that even if he succeeds in issuing the order, the new president can overturn it. Knowing this, the Pentagon will stall until after the January 20 inauguration."

"So, at your next meeting with your source, you can tell him this?"

"Yes. And that just might dampen the Taliban's wishful thinking that the Americans are going home.

"Changing the subject. As you know, headquarters has this standing requirement with us that we check the local hospitals every now and then to see how they're handling the Coronavirus. Yesterday I visited the Sardar Mohammad Dawood Khan hospital. That's one of the largest in Kabul, six floors, with the second floor devoted to Covid-19 patients. I had to sign a certificate claiming I had been tested within the past 48 hours—which was true, by the way—and after donning a mask one of the male nurses led me through the second floor. He told me they only accept fifteen patients at a time and four of those are on ventilators. Two days ago three of those patients died and were taken to the local morgue. They're very concerned lest a corpse infect others before it can be moved."

"Sounds awful. Is that worth a report to headquarters?"

"Not yet. I'll wait a day or two, make another visit, and we'll go from there."

"In the meantime, Art, I think it's time for both of us to learn more about the Taliban. We all know the organization is the world's worst—if that's the right word—terrorist organization. But if we're going to be interacting with local Afghans who fear this group, we should know as much as they do, maybe more. There's a lot of info available on the Internet, so let's have a look there, first."

* * *

Ten days later, the two men prepared a detailed report, reflecting what they had learned.

'The Taliban refer to themselves as the Islamic Emirate of Afghanistan. It is a Sunni Islamic fundamentalist political movement and military organization, currently waging war—an insurgency or *jihad*—within the country. Since 2016 the organization's leader is Mawlawi Hibatullah Akhundzada

'From 1996 to 2001, the Taliban held power over roughly three quarters of Afghanistan and enforced a strict interpretation of *Sharia* or Islamic law. The Taliban emerged in 1994 as one of the prominent factions in the Afghan Civil War and largely consisted of students from the Pashtun of eastern and southern Afghanistan who had been educated in traditional Islamic schools, and fought during the Soviet-Afghan war. Under the leadership of Mohammed Omar, the movement spread throughout most of Afghanistan, sequestering power from the Mujahideen warlords.

'The totalitarian Islamic Emirate of Afghanistan was established in 1996 and the Afghan capital was transferred to Kandahar. It held control of most of the country until being overthrown after the American-led invasion of Afghanistan in December 2001 following the September 11 attacks. At its peak, formal diplomatic recognition of the Taliban's government was acknowledged by only three nations: Pakistan, Saudi Arabia and the United Arab Emirates.. The group later regrouped as an insurgency movement to fight the American-backed Karzai administration and the NATO-led international Security Assistance Force in the war in Afghanistan.

'The Taliban have been condemned internationally for the harsh enforcement of their interpretation of Islamic Sharia law, which has resulted in the brutal treatment of many Afghans, especially women [During their rule from 1996 to 2001, the Taliban and their allies committed massacres against Afghan civilians, denied UN food supplies to 160,000 starving civilians and conducted a policy of scorched earth, burning vast areas of fertile land and destroying tens of thousands of homes. During their rule they banned hobbies and activities such as kite flying and keeping birds as pets, and indiscriminately targeted many ethnic minorities, including Shiite Muslims, while their enforcement of identifiable badges on Hindus was likened to Nazi Germany's treatment of Jews. According to the United Nations, the Taliban and their allies were responsible for 76% of Afghan civilian casualties in 2010, 80% in 2011, and 80% in 2012. The Taliban has also engaged in cultural genocide, destroying numerous monuments including the famous 1500-year old Buddhas of Bamiyan.

'The Taliban's ideology has been described as combining an innovative form of sharia Islamic law based Deobandi fundamentalism and the militant Islamism and Salafi jihadism of Osama bin Laden with Pashtun social and cultural norms known as Pashtunwali, as most Taliban are Pashtun tribesmen.

'The Pakistani Inter-Services Intelligence and military are widely alleged by the international community and the Afghan government to have provided support to the Taliban during their founding and time in power, and of continuing to support the Taliban during the insurgency. The Pakistani government claims that it dropped all support for the group after Osama bin Laden's nine-eleven attacks In 2001.

'When the Taliban took power in 1996, twenty years of continuous warfare had devastated Afghanistan's infrastructure economy. There was no running water, little electricity, few telephones, functioning roads or regular energy supplies. Basic necessities like water, food, housing and others were in desperately short supply. In addition, the clan and family structure that provided Afghans with a social/economic safety net was also badly damaged. Afghanistan's infant mortality was the highest in the world. A full quarter of all children died before they reached their fifth birthday, a rate several times higher than most other developing countries.

'International charitable and/or development organizations (NGOs) were extremely important to the supply of food, employment, reconstruction, and other services, but the Taliban proved highly suspicious toward the 'help' those groups offered. With one million plus deaths during the years of war, the number of families headed by widows had reached 98,000 by 1998. In Kabul, where vast portions of the city had been devastated by rocket attacks, more than half of its 1.2 million people benefited in some way from NGO activities, even for drinking water. The civil war and its never-ending refugee stream continued throughout the Taliban's reign. The Mazar, Herat, and Shomalil valley offensives displaced more than three-quarters of a million civilians, using "scorched earth" tactics to prevent them from supplying the enemy with aid.

'Taliban decision-makers, particularly Mullah Omar, seldom if ever talked directly to non-Muslim foreigners, so aid providers had to deal with intermediaries whose approvals and agreements were often reversed. Around September 1997 the heads of three UN agencies in Kandahar were expelled from the country after protesting when a female attorney for the UN High Commissioner for Refugees was forced to talk from behind a curtain so her face would not be visible.

'The Taliban were largely founded by Pakistan's ISI (its Inter-services Intelligence agency), beginning in 1994; the I.S.I. used the Taliban to establish a regime in Afghanistan which would be favorable to Pakistan, as they were trying to gain strategic depth. Since the creation of the Taliban, the ISI and the Pakistani military have given financial, logistical and military support.

'According to Pakistani Afghanistan expert Ahmed Rashid, "between 1994 and 1999, an estimated 80,000 to 100,000 Pakistanis trained and fought in Afghanistan" on the side of the Taliban. Another well-placed observer stated that up until 9/11 Pakistani military and ISI officers along with thousands of regular Pakistani armed forces personnel had been involved in the fighting in Afghanistan.

'During 2001, according to several international sources, 28,000–30,000 Pakistani nationals, 14,000–15,000 Afghan Taliban and 2,000–3,000 al Qaeda militants were fighting against anti-Taliban forces in Afghanistan as a roughly 45,000 strong military force. Pakistani President Pervez Musharraf—then serving as Chief of Army Staff—was responsible for sending thousands of Pakistanis to fight alongside the Taliban and Bin Laden against the forces of Ahmad Shah Massoud. Of the estimated 28,000 Pakistani nationals fighting in Afghanistan, 8,000 were militants recruited in Islamic schools, thus filling regular Taliban ranks. The document further states that the parents of those Pakistani nationals "know nothing regarding their child's military involvement with the Taliban until their bodies are brought back to Pakistan".

'A 1998 document by the U. S. State Department confirms that "20–40 percent of Taliban soldiers are Pakistani." According to the State Department report and reports by Human Rights Watch, the other Pakistani nationals fighting in Afghanistan were regular Pakistani soldiers from the army, providing direct combat support.

'Human Rights Watch wrote in 2000: Of all the foreign powers involved in efforts to sustain and manipulate the ongoing fighting [in Afghanistan], Pakistan is distinguished both by the sweep of its objectives and the scale of its efforts, which include soliciting funding for the Taliban, bankrolling Taliban operations, providing diplomatic support as the Taliban's virtual emissaries abroad, arranging training for Taliban fighters, recruiting skilled and unskilled manpower to serve in Taliban armies, planning and directing offensives, providing and facilitating shipments of ammunition and fuel, and providing combat support.

'On 1 August 1997, the Taliban launched an attack on Sheberghan, the main military base of Abdul Rashid Dostum. Dostum has said the reason the attack was successful was due to 1500 Pakistani commandos taking part and that the Pakistani air force also gave support.

'In 1998, Iran accused Pakistan of sending its air force to bomb Mazar-i-Sharif in support of Taliban forces and directly accused Pakistani troops for "war crimes at Bamiyan. The same year, Russia said Pakistan was responsible for the "military expansion" of the Taliban in northern Afghanistan by sending large numbers of Pakistani troops, some of whom had subsequently been taken as prisoners by the anti-Taliban United Front.

'During 2000, the UN Security Council imposed an arms embargo against military support to the Taliban, with UN officials explicitly singling out Pakistan. The UN secretary-general implicitly criticized Pakistan for its military support and the Security Council stated it was "deeply distress[ed] over reports of involvement in the fighting, on the Taliban side, of thousands of non-Afghan nationals". In July 2001, several countries, including the United States, accused Pakistan of being "in violation of U.N. sanctions because of its military aid to the Taliban". The Taliban also obtained financial resources from Pakistan. In 1997 alone, after Kabul was overrun by the Taliban, Pakistan gave $30 million in aid and a further $10 million for government wages.

'During 2000, British Intelligence (MI-6) reported that the ISI was taking an active role in several Al-Qaeda training camps. The ISI helped with the construction of training camps for both the Taliban and Al-Qaeda. From 1996 to 2001 Osama bin Laden and Ayman al- Zawahiri's Al-Qaeda became a state within the Taliban state.

'The role of the Pakistani military has been described by international observers as well as by the anti-Taliban leader Ahmad Shah Massoud as a "creeping invasion."'

*　*　*

"Interesting stuff, Art, and it confirms what we've thought all along. The Pakistani government is trying to have it both ways. It's been nine years since Seal Team Six killed bin Ladin at his fortress-home in Abbottabad, something the Paks knew nothing about and even if they had, they couldn't have done anything about it."

"True. But with al Qaeda pretty much out of the way, now we've got the Taliban to worry about, as we've just learned. The next time I see Amin I'll ask him if he has any stories that describe just how awful these Taliban people really are. We know they treat their women like slaves, but it would be good to have an eye witness account."

* * *

Over the following four weeks, DCOS Arthur Waite met with informant Amin Kalhan a number of times, each meeting a continuation of the previous one. Waite's report reads as follows and, owing to its importance, is likely to be come part of the Kabul station's archives.

* * *

'Benesh Sayed is a 28 year old employee of the American Embassy in Kabul. She speaks her native language Pashto as well as American English which she learned at Kabul's American University. She is one of a four-person female group which assists American embassy personnel with shopping, travel and restaurant reservations and theater tickets. Her group works in the embassy's street-level suite of offices, along side the consular offices. These facilities are open to the public because their work is not classified.

'One of the regular visitors to this group is Amir Muhammad, a junior officer in Afghanistan's Ministry of Foreign Affairs. Like Benesh, Amir speaks Pasto and American English. Although a junior officer, Amir's keen knowledge of English has prompted his supervisors to designate him as the official liaison officer between the American embassy and Afghanistan's MFA.

'Like Benesh, Amir is single, as he says to himself, 'On my meager government income, there's no way I can afford to be dating.' But not so with Benesh. She lives with her widowed mother in a small apartment, in one of the city's poorer districts, a two floor walk-up, no elevator and plumbing that works, most of the time. Her mother suffers from diabetes and, like most elderly Afghan women, she has no health insurance, relying on her daughter's income to pay for her prescription drugs.

'Amir visits the American embassy at least once a week and, recently, he has been taking time to chat with Benesh. He thinks of it as 'official business,' but he finds Benesh attractive, a good conversationalist and not at all timid about being seen with a man. After his third visit Amir asks Benesh if she'd be willing to have dinner with him in a nearby restaurant. He knows that her father no longer lives with his family, and so she doesn't have to get permission to accept Amir's invitation. Benesh agrees and Amir chooses the *Serena,* one of Kabul's finest.

'There is some risk here, and the two know it. The restaurant's waiters will wonder how it is that these two are here without a chaperone, and obviously very much into each other. Perhaps worse, Amir orders two vodka martinis, knowing full well that in the Islamic culture alcohol is forbidden. But Amir also knows that the Serena's clientele includes as many foreigners as it does the local citizenry, and management is more than happy to treat everyone the same. For some time, the management has insisted that its patrons wear masks and the tables are arranged according to the accepted social distancing rules.'

* * *

"So, Benesh, we see that the menu is printed in both English and Pashto. It offers several choices and I would recommend the lamb Shish kebab. It comes with asparagus tips in Bearnaise sauce and French Fries."

"Whatever you say, Amir. You know more about this than I do,"

"What would your mother say if we ordered a cocktail?"

"She's not here, is she?"

"No. So let's try a vodka martini. Have you ever had one?"

"Goodness, no! I've never drunk any kind of alcohol. It's forbidden in our culture. You surely know that."

"Of course I do. But this restaurant caters to people from all over the world, it's international. And, besides, one martini won't matter, after you've finished eating."

* * *

'After that first martini, Amir persuaded Benesh to have a glass of white wine, a perfect complement to the Shish kebab.

'Following dinner and coffee the two walked out of the restaurant—each of them a little unsteady—and toward the parking stall where Amir's 2015 Russian *Lada* automobile was waiting. Ever the gentleman, Amir took Benesh's right hand in his. She looked up at him and smiled her approval.

"That was a perfect evening, Amir, let's do it again, soon."

*   *   *

'*Unbeknownst to either of them, Murad Natirbov, the Taliban's precinct captain, had a clear view of the couple, holding hands, smiling and laughing, as they approached the Lada. He reported this sighting to his superior, Abdul Malik, who in turn reported it to Imam Omar Abdul. Abdul's mosque is the worship center for about thirty percent of Kabul's Muslim population and the man has much influence. After considering the report, he decided to issue a fatwa, condemning the woman for appearing in public without a male relative alongside.*

*   *   *

'The Haji Muhammad mosque publishes a weekly newsletter for its worshippers and each of its articles is reviewed by Omar Abdul to ensure accuracy and sufficient detail. Sometimes it scolds the worshippers for failing to wear masks, especially when they are shaking hands with the imam who refuses to wear a mask, asserting that if Allah wanted him to wear a mask, he would have said so.

'In the Saturday issue, following his awareness of the woman's indiscretion, he published his *fatwa,* declaring her an apostate who must be punished according to Sharia law. Depending on the severity of the offense, punishment could include death by stoning or a lifetime prison sentence. He chose the latter, citing Prophet Muhammad's many statements about seeking Allah's mercy and forgiveness.

* * *

Amin Kalhan has finished reading the imam's article. He reaches for his iPhone and taps the 'emergency' icon. Seconds later, I respond.

"What's up, Friend? Is this really an emergency?"

"I think you'll agree that it is. Here's the story.

'I just finished reading a newsletter article written by imam Omar Abdul. He's the leader of one of the city's largest mosques. The article identifies our Benesh Sayed as an apostate, guilty—without a trial, mind you—and sentenced to a lifetime in prison. This Abdul guy has the authority to do that so you people should move quickly."

"How many know about this?"

"Everyone who reads that newsletter, at least several hundred."

"Well, the press will be on this within hours and it'll probably make news just about everywhere. We need to talk to Benesh, here in my office. She'll be safe here and we can put her up in one of our guest apartments. That will give us time to notify headquarters and we can work up a plan to make sure she'll be okay for a very long time."

"Sounds good. Next steps?"

"I'll get a message off to headquarters and we'll see if they approve what I have in mind. We should know within the next twelve hours."

* * *

Terry Bannister, chief of the Afghan desk at CIA headquarters, was the first to see Arthur White's message and he immediately recognized its potential. Although unstated, it had long been U.S. government policy to publicly embarrass the Taliban by any means available. He sent an interoffice email to CIA director Miriam Jefferson and she immediately gave him a thumbs up, saying this was exactly what president Oglethorpe had hoped for. Bannister's people in Kabul would be pleased.

* * *

"Just what we wanted, Dick. Amin's never been to the embassy but on my say-so, they'll let him come inside, just long enough to locate Benesh and tell her what we have in mind."

"Okay, Art, go for it!"

* * *

Benesh is sitting in her accustomed place with her three colleagues. She immediately recognizes Amin.

"Amin! What are *you* doing here?"

"Believe it or not, Benesh, I'm acting as representative of the United States government, so listen up."

"Yes, please!"

"We know about your *situation* with imam Abdul and I'm sure you do too."

"Of course, and I'm scared to death."

"Well, you needn't be. We've received word from Washington that you're eligible for political asylum, given what you've been through. That means that, for starters, you're to stay right here in the embassy building. There's a fully-equipped guest apartment that will be your home for as along as it takes for you to leave Afghanistan. You're not safe here, as you know."

"Do I have a choice?"

"Certainly. Why do you ask?"

"Because I have friends in London, a group of people who live there, among others who have fled Afghanistan. I believe they're called *expatriates.*"

"That's perfect, Benesh. One of the embassy's consular officers can get your exit visa. You'll have to fill out some forms, sign them and then he'll do the rest. And our embassy in London will see to it that you'll be welcome. If you'll give me the names and addresses of your friends we'll forward that info to our people in London."

"Yes, Amin, but it would even more *perfect* if you were to join me. We might even fall in love and that would be a good thing."

*   *   *

Iman Omar Abdul is saying goodbye to those worshippers who are filing out of his Haji Muhammad mosque. As the last one leaves, he turns and says to his assistant.

"Mustafa, my friend. I'm not feeling very well so if you're willing I should like you to do our service next Friday."

"Certainly, Most Excellent, I should be glad to do that. Is there anything I can do for you?"

"No, but thank you. I'd prefer you not repeat this but I'm afraid I might have been infected by this Coronavirus. As you know, I've never been persuaded that wearing a mask is helpful and I shake hands with so many people - - - that's what I'm afraid has happened."

Ten days later imam Omar Abdul died, his last words thanking Allah for allowing him so many years of faithful service.

* * *

As happens, the international press rarely misses a good story. An American reporter for *The Wall Street Journal*—the only one in Kabul—somehow learned of imam Omar Abdul's fatwa that would have sent Benesh Sayed to prison for life. His article appeared the next morning, together with a photo of Benesh, and the results were predictable. The Internet suddenly was filled with articles demanding that the imam be sent to prison, or worse. Leaders of France, Germany and Italy demanded that the case be brought before the International Court of Justice in The Hague.

The American embassy in London issued a statement saying that Benesh Sayed was about to arrive in London where she would be among friends, and that she would be granted British citizenship if she wished to do so.

* * *

Three weeks later Benesh Sayed *and* Amin Kalhan arrived at Heathrow Airport. They were greeted by a small group of Afghan expatriates and whisked away to their new apartment. The couple will live together for as long as it takes them to acquire British citizenship, then, if all goes well, they will become man and wife.

* * *

CIA Chief of Station Richard Lawson and his deputy Arthur White are having lunch in the embassy's cafeteria.

"You know, Art, thinking about how the imam died, I recall hearing a sermon a long time ago and the preacher ended it by saying that 'God works His will in mysterious ways.' That's probably what happened here."

TEN

From Wikipedia:

Miami's Gesu Catholic church is significant for its important role in the religious history of Miami and as a reflection of the city's growth and development. The buildings are excellent examples of religious architecture and noteworthy for the excellence of its design, craftsmanship, and detailing.

Gesu is Miami's oldest Catholic parish and has served the religious and humanitarian needs of the community for more than a century. The growth of the parish closely parallels the development of the City of Miami.

Miami's first Catholic Mass was conducted in 1872 by Bishop John Marcellus and confirmed the pioneer family of William J. Wagner. Wagner constructed a small wooden church on his homestead in 1875, and this became Miami's first house of worship.

The Holy Name Parish (now Gesu) was organized in 1896 and the pastor was Father Ambrose Fontan, S.J. A new church was constructed in 1897 on land donated by Henry Flagler. As Miami's population and the Holy Name congregation expanded, the need for a larger church became evident. A cornerstone was subsequently laid on December 10, 1920, on the site of the earlier church, and the new building was dedicated in 1925. The Gesu Parish School opened in 1905 with six grades and 60 students. The original school name was The Academy of the Sisters of St. Joseph St. Catherine's Convent. The school was also known as St. Catherine's Convent School and St. Catherine's Academy. There were four graduates in the first high school graduating class of 1913. The Sisters of St. Joseph of St. Augustine, Florida, were the teaching staff at the school.

A new five story school was built in 1926 and the name changed to Gesu Parish School. It was located at 130 Northeast 2nd Street. The last Gesu High School graduation was in 1953. There were 40 graduates in that class. The last eighth grade graduation was in 1982 when the school was closed. The school was demolished in 1984.

Gesu Church continues to serve as one of the three downtown churches and was recently restored to its original appearance. The parish has been staffed by the Jesuits of Antilles province since 2004. Previously it was staffed by the Jesuits of New Orleans province. The church seating capacity is 700 plus 150 in choir balcony.

* * *

Fr Samuel Ordonez knew that most of his parishioners would want to participate. It would be a virtual service, in keeping with the governor's rules about dealing with the Coronavirus. Nearly all of his flock had computers or iPhones, so very few would miss out. It would be a memorial service like none other, celebrating the life of a man who had changed the economic and cultural landscape of South Florida. José Martinez had for years been a household word, not only in Miami but throughout the state. Born in a suburb of Havana in 1929, he became an orphan at age eight when his parents died in a house fire. He lived with relatives for two years and then his uncle paid the captain of a large trawler to take the lad to Miami where distant relatives would care for him. In the United States the Great Depression was well underway and the U.S. immigration authorities had little interest in preventing the admission of one more Cuban child.

José's relatives, a distant aunt and uncle, made sure the child learned to speak English as soon as he was able and by age six he was fluent in both Spanish and English. And he was an exceptional student, moving through his first six grades with ease. High school was the same and he graduated with at 3.5 gpa. Then, on to Miami's Florida International University, were he graduated, in 1950, with a degree in agricultural management. Why such an interest?

José had done his homework. He knew that Florida was already the nation's leading producer of citrus, oranges and grapefruit and he also knew that his aunt and uncle were owners of 75 acres of undeveloped land, about five miles from their home. He procured a loan of $45,000 from the Farm Credit Bureau—a holdover agency from the Roosevelt years and the Great Depression—hired a three-man crew—and began the arduous task of planting 2,000 orange tree seedlings

Now, the waiting began. On average, the seedling needs about three years before it grows enough to bear fruit. During this period the plant needs plenty of water and lots of sunshine, each available in sunny south Florida.

During those three years José and his crew made sure the plants were properly cared for but they also wanted to expand their circle of friends within their community. Their temporary home was in Coconut Grove, expensive but affordable, with two Catholic churches to choose from.

And it was during this hiatus that he met, fell in love with and married Maria Sanchez, herself a former Cuban national and now a United States citizen. Within three years the couple had produced one son, Roberto and a daughter, Margarita.

* * *

As the years passed, José realized that he didn't know enough about the citrus fruit industry to take advantage of its potential. So he contacted his professors at FIU and after several learning sessions he began to invest in *Florida Fruit and Produce,* the country's largest of its kind, and listed on the NASDAQ exchange as FFP. Over the next ten years, his investments had made him a wealthy man, wealthy enough to retire and turn over the management of his empire to his son Roberto. But not content to 'do nothing' in his retirement, José incorporated himself into a 501(c)(3) charitable trust and named it *Martinez Management*. He sought doners from all over the country, brought on a board of directors, and within five years the trust had accumulated more than $100,000,000. Many of the contributors were—like himself—Cuban-Americans, some of whom maintained ties to relatives in Cuba. The charities included The American Red Cross, March of Dimes, the American Alzheimer's Association, Boys' Town, The Salvation Army and The Martinez Mission, a newly re-named hospital in Coconut Grove.

* * *

By age 18, Roberto had tired of leading Martinez Management and with his father's permission handed the reins to his sister Margarita. During his growing up years he decided the citrus fruit industry was not something he wanted to be part of. Toward that end he attended the University of Florida's law school and five years later took the state's bar exam, which he passed on his first try. One of his professors had recommended that he apply to a firm peopled by Spanish-speaking attorneys and that is what he did, landing his first job as an intern in the Miami law firm of Lopez, Garcia, Morales and Perez. The firm's senior partner, Juan Lopez, wanted someone bilingual in Spanish and English, with a passion for helping Spanish-speaking immigrants.

Over the following five years, Roberto had become the go-to lawyer whenever the firm found itself in court defending one of the region's many Spanish-speaking citizens: divorce, child abandonment, tax evasion, even kidnapping. His reputation was enhanced by a number of articles, with photographs, appearing in the local print media and on television.

* * *

One day, in the office of Juan Lopez

"Roberto, the partners and I have decided that your track record is well-enough known that you should consider getting into politics, here in Miami. As you may know, the mayor appoints a City Manager who is in fact the man who runs the city's various departments. It's a powerful position and the pay isn't bad. You're a solid Conservative, as are the rest of us, and it would help the firm's reputation if you were to do what I'm recommending. What do you think?"

"I'm flattered beyond measure, Juan. But I've got to be up front about this. I'm about to be married - - -"

"You what?!"

"Yes, Maria and I have been in love for a very long time but we thought it was nobody's business but ours and that's why we haven't said anything. The wedding is just two weeks away and we'll need two weeks for a honeymoon and after that I'm good to go."

"Hmm. Well, okay, Roberto. We'll be sorry to lose you but we can live with that. And congratulations!"

* * *

The wedding was a quiet one, the few guests were close friends, each wearing a mask and observing the social distancing rules. Though it was expensive, the couple decided to hold the event in Miami's historic Gesu Catholic church, bishop Thomas Maloney presiding. Even so, none of those present were aware that Maria was three months pregnant. It was a personal thing, she thought, and no one need know, other than Roberto. They eventually named their beautiful seven pound daughter Alexa, anticipating—as all new parents do—that she would one day become something special.

* * *

The city's leading newspaper, *The Miami Herald,* told its many readers that—in the opinion of its editorial board—Roberto Gonzalez' appointment was the most flagrant political stunt in the city's history. The man's few years as a lawyer in no way qualifies him for one of the city's most important positions. His inherited wealth no doubt was an important consideration in his selection, and readers should expect evidence to emerge that he will use this wealth to *buy* those favors so necessary in the life of any politician.

Roberto considered himself thick-skinned enough to endure the hostility, which he hoped would soon evaporate. Not so with his wife, Maria. Within hours of reading the Herald's editorial, three of the city's television outlets were beaming the same story, with photographs. The woman was devastated and her first concern was for her unborn child.

"Sweetheart! What will the neighbors think? Is it safe to go out?"

"Not to worry, Maria. Our neighbors are a conservative group. That's why we chose this neighborhood. If anything, they're likely to take our side."

"I hope you're right. Baby Alexa is due next month and we don't need any more of this publicity. Doctor Rodriguez told me I should ignore it, try to stay quiet and get plenty of rest."

* * *

Baby Alexa was born as obstetrician Rodrigues predicted, but by Caesarean Section. He advised the proud parents that it would be wise for them not to try for another child. With proper attention and care she should grow to be a beautiful young woman, sharing the DNA of her parents.

* * *

And so it was. By the time Alexa was a senior at Miami's Jackson High School her peers and teachers thought of her as an outstanding example of a young woman who, if left to her own devices, would make a difference in her community. She was pretty, from a wealthy family, an excellent student with an obvious sympathy for those not so fortunate. And, she was modest. She never spoke of her family's wealth, she wanted to be treated like everyone else in her class.

After graduating from Jackson High, Alexa chose to move on to Miami's Florida International University. One of the largest public universities in the United States, FIU's student population represented more than139 countries. Many of its classes were taught in both English and Spanish, a few in German, French and Italian. Alexa's Spanish-speaking teachers tried to treat her like any other student, but it was obvious to them that, on graduation, she would much more than just another graduate.

Alexa did not disappoint. She graduated with a 3.75 gpa and a degree in Community Service.

*   *   *

One month after her graduation, Alexa is in her father's office, seeking his ideas about something she has been considering for some time.

"Papa, now that you've had this job as City Manager for a while, I have an idea I'd like to talk about."

"Sure, Alexa, go ahead."

"Yes. It doesn't take a genius to know that our city has an enormous homeless problem. Sure there are, what, twenty or so homeless shelters scattered here and there? But they're under-funded, the residents—many of them—are on drugs, and nothing seems to change."

"Yes, Sweetheart, I'm well aware of this. But most of the financing is voluntary, from, say, The Salvation Army or Samaritan's Purse or the American Red Cross. And that means the city can't do much to help."

"Okay. I get that. But what about *private* financing? I mean, our family has enough money to help, and help a great deal."

"Hmm, yes, I suppose you're right. Any ideas?"

"Sure, I've been thinking about this for months. Let's say we establish a privately-funded shelter. We make it known that this shelter is *only* for indigent Spanish-speaking residents and those few immigrants who are still making their way from Cuba. We could even give it a name, say, the Martinez Mission."

"I like that, Alexa. But you'll need a license. It won't cost much but you need it, to be legal."

"Can't you do that, for me?"

"I can, but nepotism is frowned on."

"What if we do it quietly? No one needs to know."

"That will work, until the shelter is up and running. Then everyone will know."

* * *

Ten months later the Martinez Mission was a legal, licensed homeless shelter with an initial population of 86, 48 men and 38 women. It provided three meals a day with individual apartments for married couples and single rooms for those without spouses. It was located in one of Miami's poorer neighborhoods, locally referred to as *Minimum Miami*. Admittance required a test for Covid-19 with a 14-day quarantine for those testing positive. Unlike many shelters this one operated on an honor system. Residents were free to come and go but each was warned that using drugs would mean ejection from the shelter.

As with most shelters, there soon developed a kind of hierarchy, wherein one person became the 'head man.' Hector Riaz, 28 and single, quickly became the most popular person. He was fluent in both English and Spanish and handsome enough to generate admiring glances from a few of the younger women. But Hector had another life, something he dared not share. He was a drug dealer and his supplier was a man—Hector never knew his real name—who headed a local travel agency which gave him natural access to those with enough money to book passage anywhere in the world. Most of this was done online and his customers knew they had to wait until the Coronavirus vaccine was available. Still, it was profitable enterprise, known only to Hector and his online customers.

One of these customers was Jeremy Wallace, the equipment manger for the Miami Dolphins football team. Jerry, as the team called him, was an impatient man. He visited Hector and asked if he could have just a half-ounce of marijuana. Yes, but he'd have to buy it from one of Hector's customers, a jeweler who had a shop not far from the shelter. Unfortunately for Hector, the jeweler was an unaware asymptomatic carrier of the Coronavirus pathogen. And, sure enough, during one of the team's late August practice sessions, starting left tackle Bruce Albright—a second year first round draft choice out of Texas A & M—became infected. According to NFL rules, then and now, every player, all the coaches and other linked to the team, are required to take the Covid-19 test. When Albright's infection became known, the team had no choice: cancel at least three of its upcoming games.

A serious blow. The Dolphins were in second place in the AFC East division, one game behind the Buffalo Bills, their next game scheduled for the following Sunday. That crucial meeting had to be canceled, much to the everlasting dismay of both Miami and Buffalo fans. The same for two more games with the New England Patriots and New York Jets.

* * *

As most Americans are aware, life will return to normal, including professional football, when the long-awaited vaccine is available to everyone—which at the time of writing may be only a few months off—until then, each of us must wait and see.

EPILOGUE

This story began on January 1, 2020, a few days after the novel Coronavirus escaped from a laboratory in Wuhan, China. It was first recognized, and reported, by an aspiring physician, Zhang Wei Ying. Zhang Wei recognized the seriousness of what had happened but he was powerless to do anything about it. The rulers in far-off Beijing had little or no interest in what had happened. But, within days, the Chinese Communist government orchestrated a massive coverup, denying the seriousness of the outbreak and insisting their country had had nothing to do with it. Further, they asserted, pathogens such as the Coronavirus transfer *only* from one animal to another, never to humans.

This assertion, of course, was dismissed as clumsy propaganda by nearly every medical expert on the planet. Still, the Chinese continued their denial and, in some respects, they still do.

As we all know, today China's Communist leaders seek to establish political and economic hegemony over the entire world. And they are very good at what they do.

As an author, I can only hope that my examples of the destructive power of the novel Coronavirus will give readers an opportunity to consider what they might do to avoid the infection, not only for themselves but for their neighbors as well.

John Sager
January, 2021

ABOUT THE AUTHOR

John Sager is a retired United States intelligence officer whose services for the CIA, in various capacities, spanned more than a half-century. A widower, he makes his home in the Covenant Shores retirement community on Mercer Island, Washington.

©Yuen Lui Studio, 2003

Printed in the United States
By Bookmasters